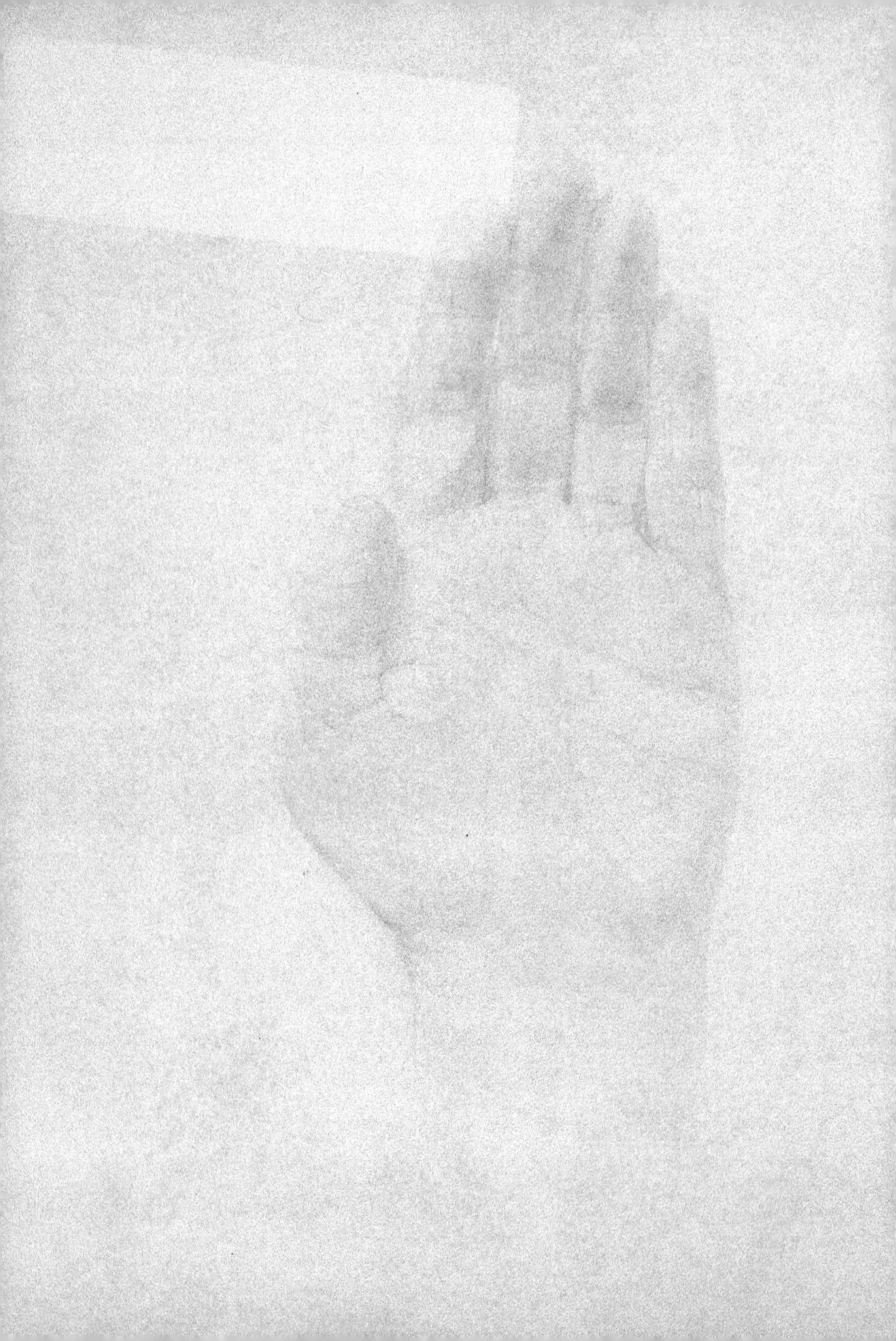

HANDS ON A MIRROR

Owen Hill

Bootstrap Press
2021

 / ISBN 13: 978-1-946741-09-7

Earlier versions of these pieces appeared in the following publications: "Union Steward" in *Decentralized Publication #17: Printed and Bound in Solidarity*; "F. A. Nettelbeck" in *Poetry Flash*; "Patti Smith" in *AMERARCANA #7: Shuffle Boil Special Issue*; and "Clifford Still" in *Try*.

Thanks and love to Noah Ross, for his encouragement, and for helping me turn these fugitive pieces into a book. And, always and forever, to Liz and Zelda.

Cover art by Colter Jacobsen. Interior illustration by Colter Jacobsen, 2019: "don't let your right hand know what your left hand is going through (Lungfish)"

Typesetting and book design by Impart Ink

Bootstrap Press books are edited by Derek Fenner and Ryan Gallagher.
www.bootstrappress.org

Fee Dawson (1930-2002)

Union Steward

I was nineteen when I was elected union steward. Brotherhood of Railway and Airline Clerks. I had been hired out of high school to work in baggage service, checking claim stubs, tearing the tickets off bags, filling out lost luggage forms, taking guff from bagless passengers. After that first wave of hijackings—mid-seventies—the FAA had x-rays and metal detectors put in. The airlines needed cheap labor to run the operation. They hired fly-by-night security companies to handle things, then bought the companies and gutted them. For the cost of a few cheap blazers, some minimum wage workers and a couple of managers they could check bags well enough to satisfy the FAA. The old baggage service crew was laid off, but we were told that we could apply for jobs with the new company. Lower wage, cheaper suit, more work, no benefits. The last cut was the hardest. We lost our flight discounts.

I wasn't real employable and needed something that fit with my school schedule—so I re-applied, picked up my cheap red blazer, and became a PSR (passenger service representative is what they called us). This meant spending half my shift in front of an x-ray machine, looking for weapons. I had never seen a real weapon, and the training session was an hourlong joke. A bunch of us shared a joint beforehand, hiding behind that stupid looking restaurant in the LAX parking lot. We were the first wave in the anti-terrorist army.

I reported for work at 6pm and worked 'till 3am. An interesting time to be in an airport. It was tough work early in the shift. Lots of flights, lines of cranky tired people. After midnight there were two flights, outgoing to Dallas and incoming from

JFK. A quiet airport is a strange and noirish place. I liked it, then, romanticizing everything like you do at that age. A crew of about fifty covered all the shifts at Terminal 4. A ragtag group. I remember being shocked, and I have to say a little excited that there were so many ex-cons. Wasn't there a screening process? I got along well with them. They were earnest, and, understandably, afraid of getting fired. Most of them were taking classes, nursing, business, the trades. They were surprisingly respectful of my literary pretensions—they loved poetry, or at least the idea of poetry. Odd that it was a place where I felt perfectly comfortable being a poet, unlike the office and retail jobs that followed. There was another faction on the staff—people who wanted to go up the ladder, become flight attendants and ticket agents, then move into management. They didn't have a chance. It was like jumping from semi-pro softball to the major leagues. Management didn't take us seriously—they saw us as a drain on profits, part of a boondoggle, a product of government regulation. Who needs the FAA? And they knew we were various brands of loser—Junior College students, ex-cons, older folks who couldn't afford retirement, artsy types. All the same to them.

If you do something every day you find a way to take pride. With no help from management, we got to know the x-ray machines. A dark bar at the bottom of the screen could possibly be a knife, especially if it showed lighter at one end. A co-worker with an interest in guns tutored me on the various types, shapes and sizes. We developed a system of signals, mostly to identify troublesome passengers. This wasn't discussed, but over time I guess people decided that it was just better to do a decent job. I've seen it a lot in my working life—an esprit de corps that develops at the low end of the pay scale. Helps make things tolerable. Management tries to promote that, of course, with their pizza days and casual Fridays but when it's fake it's fake and everybody knows it. I didn't, still don't, like the idea of working in law enforcement but this seemed different. Who wants guns on an airplane? We moved the passengers through quickly and we confiscated some weapons, and at the end of the shift when we stopped at the Jolly Roger Coffee Shop we felt OK about the work.

If you work for a living you experience these clampdowns. A new middle-manager, a drop in profits, or just somebody bored at the top—the reasons are often a mystery to the working stiff. It's like a stretch of bad weather, it passes but when it does things are a little worse than before. This guy had one of those typically ambiguous titles—call him Operations Manager. I imagine now that he had a military background—just back from Vietnam? The time would be about right. It wasn't my first experience with the breed. In high school I worked frying tortillas at the local Taco Bell. My manager was a typical dumbass spit and polish type. One morning, after giving the prep crew some shit about shining fixtures, he had a war flashback fueled breakdown. Should have burned that draft card.

Our new Operations Manager was a little more polished on the surface but also kind of brittle. He fired a couple of people in his first month, picking off people who weren't quite making the grade. Flexing his muscles. Then he hired a few people who seemed like old friends. Not really a strategy, just something that you expect out of a new boss. We complained amongst ourselves, and at first it didn't go anywhere. Then things got closer to home. Good people were fired. People we counted on to show up and get the job done, friends. The airlines lost money and the company was fined a few hundred thousand for making illegal campaign donations—bad economy, bad publicity, nervous execs. Layoffs without notice or severance, increased workload, if you work you've been through it.

I'd like to say that my entry into union organizing came from some deep concern for the worker, or that I had worked out some sort of Marxist based philosophy, but, really I did it for love. The woman I was living with was in a car accident. Not too serious, but scary. I called in sick from the hospital, but I was too late. We were supposed to call in at least twenty-four hours in advance. Somebody in the personnel office transferred me to the Operations Manager, who gave me a good, military style dressing-down. I started to try and explain, then decided, what the fuck, and told him to go to hell. It felt pretty good so I elaborated a little and finished with a healthy fuck you. Didn't wait to hear "you're fired," but I assumed it would be like that.

Next evening I showed up at work, thinking it would be my last day. Somehow word had gotten out—a hero's welcome! Then a call from the office, and a ride on the employee tram out to the headquarters. I loved that ride, even if it meant going to some boring or painful meeting. The tram wound through the runways, under the wings of the big jets and the smell and the noise represented movement, world travel, escape. I felt afraid but also a little proud. An exciting job, and now I was getting fired. A true rebel.

But they didn't fire me. I think I know why now—I was a workhorse, took on extra jobs, volunteered for overtime. Mostly to cut the boredom, but also because I was green. I thought it mattered, I guess. I think their idea was to break me, make me into a valuable asset. And I was a good candidate—the supervisor sensed this. So I got off with a lecture and some sort of demerit—don't remember what system they used. Probably meant that I'd have to stay on the 3am shift, which didn't bother me.

The guy who came in with the union cards was a student at The People's Law School in LA. It really exists! He said I inspired him, but he was probably flattering me to get me on board. It worked—and it was easy to get my shift mates to sign up. The 3am shift was like the group W bench. A tough bunch. Cynical, too. They didn't expect much to come of it but they appreciated the effort. Me either, at first, but I was pissed off beyond caring. They "elected" me to represent the shift at our early meetings.

The meetings were drinking and/or smoking sessions early AM, between graveyard and the morning shift. Lots of complaining, then, what do we do now? Followed by arguments and, sometimes, agreeing to disagree. The day crew was toughest. They were itching to move up in the world. But eventually, mostly, they came around. The Op Manager had made too many enemies, and maybe they sensed that there really wasn't much for them to lose.

We didn't have to hold elections. We just needed to get a majority of the employees to sign union cards. Old law—a nineteenth century victory by the porter's union. They died for our sins—union elections are nasty affairs. Getting people to sign the cards was pretty easy. A little argument, a little bribery (free drinks), perhaps a little intimidation. Conditions were terrible and the boss was mean, so everybody was disgruntled. Still, there's this anti-union sentiment that I believe is uniquely American. "I'm not a joiner." Everybody's John Wayne. I guess that's our heritage—a blessing and a curse. American Airlines was-is-known as anti-union in the extreme. An old organizer later told me that, as a company that was founded in the south, they would always have a soft spot for the days of slavery.

We were contacted by the Brotherhood of Railway and Airline Clerks. For some reason we were allowed to have a meeting at LAX. I think the union worked this out, possibly as a way of showing their influence. We sat at a conference table in the office building. There was a coffee urn and pitchers of water. That stagnant air and those funny acoustics. Everybody looked nervous. Our union rep had just flown in from Denver, Ernie Mogg. He was too big for his suit and had a horizontal smile—kind of Buddha-like. Next to him sat the union lawyer. Can't remember his name but he was quite the stereotype.

Unlit cigar, barrel chest, red-faced. I'm not making this up. They went through some set speeches and promised a few things—raises of course, and some sort of flight benefit. They were vague on that. I arrived at the meeting a little pissed off because the manager had been riding me, had threatened to "have my job." I proposed that we not sign off on anything unless the BRAC promised to have the Operations Manager fired. To my surprise they readily agreed. I felt powerful—revenge is sweet.

Ernie and the lawyer collected our cards and just like that we're in the Brotherhood (although there were more women than men in our rank and file). Ernie told us to elect a steward and three vice stewards, one from each shift. Everybody looked at everybody else then everybody looked at me. Ernie said, "just do it now since we have a quorum. You don't need speeches. You all know each other." One of the guys with a Muslim name nominated me. He said, "they'll listen to Owen because he's white and he doesn't have a record. If I go in there we're fucked." A backhanded compliment if there ever was one but it was true.

And so I was elected. My deputies were plenty tough. A British anarchist for the day shift, a tough-as-nails dyke (haven't seen her in years but I think she'd be pleased with that description). Her brother also worked the shift, and somehow they kicked the day people into line—by intimidation, mostly. Swing shift rep was a theology student at Loyola Marymount, my introduction to lefty Christianity. He was soft spoken but he was happy to fuck up management. I often wonder what happened to him. Graveyard shift belonged to my Muslim friend, who I can only remember as Gary because I met him before he went for the skinny ties, shiny shoes, short hair and wraparounds.

The airlines stalled even though the law was on our side. A few weeks went by before the union called to say that negotiations had begun and that a meeting had been planned.

The day before the meeting we were fired. Me, the vice-stewards, one of the anarchists and a couple of fellow travelers.

The Op Manager approached me as I entered the locker room. Handed me a check. TERMINATED/LAST PAYMENT stamped across the front. I almost punched him—and as I write this I wonder how that would have changed my life. Another drop of adrenalin and I would have killed him without remorse. I had never felt the weight of that kind of power structure before—at least not in a personal way. And lashing out is, I think, a sane reaction. But I guess we don't want to kill people… He had me turn in my blazer and go home. I handed it over and boarded the employee tram back to the terminal, unemployed. I stopped in baggage service to inform my comrades. Borrowed a bunch of change, went to a phone booth and called the BRAC. Stay cool, go home, wait it out. Last thing I wanted to do but I went back in, took the tram out to the lot and drove home.

Getting fired sets up a strange psychology. Even if it's management's fault, a form of intimidation, whatever, you're left with that kicked in the chest feeling. I shared an old house on the Torrance/Gardena border. We had a dog, a black lab mix and I remember walking the dog and feeling really low, then saying it's not my fault then it is/it isn't/it is. So strange, that we identify with our oppressors and give them all that power. But it happens, it's a human trait.

The union acted, fast. I got an early morning phone call from Ernie Mogg, everything was fixed, we could report to work that evening. I guess they had some muscle, back then.

I got to work a little early and one of the mechanics met me as I entered the locker room. They had threatened to walk out, and so had the Sky Caps. The place was swarming with union reps. Coming from a union family I knew about strikes but I'd never encountered this—it certainly wouldn't have happened at the Taco Bell in Redondo Beach. I clocked in and went out to baggage service and one of the Sky Caps—the union steward—shook my hand.

"You may get your tires slashed and you shouldn't take the tram alone. And record everything—write everything down!" and I have to admit that I was a little smug, didn't believe him. And I was young and felt strong—could take care of myself.

But, just like he said, next morning, 3am I'm in the Employee lot changing a tire. At least they'd only slashed one. And I was scared and didn't feel so young and strong.

They threw out their nets—that is, they enforced every rule and wrote new ones. We were ordered to clock in ten minutes early for every shift. Difficult, because the trams didn't run that often. I'd either clock in a couple of minutes late or come in half an hour early and hang around. Doesn't seem like much but if you work five days a week you don't want to waste that much time. People would try taking the later tram and running to clock in. They'd miss by a couple of minutes and find themselves on suspension, or fired. We were still negotiating a contract and it was tough to defend people while we were in that gray area. A couple of our best people just gave up, quit, and of course that played into management strategy.

I was fired, repeatedly, and I'd have to call Ernie Mogg and take the tram out to the office. Next day I'd be back on the job, but the intimidation was eating at me, at all of us. Pay checks were "lost" or "delayed" and managers from the offices staged surprise "inspections." Pro-management workers were taken out for pricey dinners and given extra vacation days for "work well done."

I was outside of baggage service on my break, hot late summer LA night, beautiful, people rushing by to catch a midnight flight to Dallas. Just enjoying the urban-ness of it all, even the scent of gas and jet fuel held some romantic mystery. All that movement! A Sky Cap came by and gave me a signal that said let's walk and smoke and we went out to the restaurant that looks like a Disney vision of some future that will never come. He lit up a joint and after he passed it he looked me in the eye and said "now you really have to watch your ass because Harlen is coming in from Chicago. He has one job in the system. He breaks unions. Listen, man: That's ALL he does. He flies around and crushes people like you. We'll back you up where we can but we're facing layoffs. We can barely keep our people. Same with the mechanics." I was young and naïve and therefore shocked, but also pissed off and as I write this years later I'm still pissed off, and I can feel the tension that I felt and that my rank and file felt that summer and fall.

If you work for a living you've felt that tension.

I feel bad that his name escapes me. Thirtyish, working class Brit accent—a young Michael Caine would play him in the movie. He had moved to LA with his sister. I don't remember what brought them over. The first anarchists I'd met—this was a couple of years before my punk period. Together they were a terror. Calling the bosses on their games, disgusted with us for being such wimps. Management put up with them, I think because of their accents. Gave the place some class. And they were white and I may as well say it—you could get away with more if you were. It was all about presenting at the airlines. Still is, but it was clunkier then. You could see the strings. The Corps are smoother now. They know how to use tokenism and when to cover their tracks. He'd clocked in late after missing the tram. The Op Manager had taken a lot of shit from him, had had it. His paycheck had been stamped Termination. But not mine, this week. I gathered up my quarters and called Denver. Funny how memory works—I still remember the phone booth, graffiti'd and stuffy in the LA heat. Ernie wasn't in but a woman on the phone gave me the rote instructions. Stay cool, send him home, wait it out. But my anarchist friend didn't want to stay cool. He wanted to take the tram out to the office and bust some heads. I couldn't physically restrain him, he was tougher than me. I suggested we go out and get a drink, cool off and make plans. I risked going home early. The shift supervisor was on the clock, pro-union so I could get away with playing sick.

We knew an unlicensed limo driver. Nice guy—we'd steer people to his car and get a five buck kickback. He drove us to a Hyatt that had a nice hotel bar. We needed to get out of LAX. My comrade was livid. I was pretty scared. I don't think "going postal" was a term we knew yet, but I feared that. I decided on a dubious strategy: I'd get him settled into the bar and feed him drinks. Of course alcohol can have any number of effects—I prayed that it would work as a sedative. He raved on and I bought the drinks. It must have cost me a week's pay, and, get this: a few weeks later Ernie had the BRAC pay me back for those drinks. I'd done the right thing.

I was trying to protect what we'd put together. I knew if we got to the office we'd rip it up, probably get arrested. Me too, because I would have felt obligated to stand with my co-worker. No questions, either. I think, once, it was in people's blood to feel loyal to co-workers. Well, many people. And I think that's a lost value now. God, I hate this—sounding like an old fart, complaining that the world has gone to hell in a handbasket, but as I try to wrestle with the decline of organized labor I keep coming up with this, that it's a character issue and something is missing, at least in the USA.

We were drinking well drinks, whatever they put in the gin and tonics. They started to do the trick. We reached that point where alcohol is a truth serum and we told our life stories. I wish I could remember the details but I think it was all pretty hardscrabble. I do remember him telling me that he liked animals better than people. He had a couple of dogs. He did have a passion for politics that came out of some love, or lost love, of humanity. I'm from a blue collar background myself so I'm loathe to romanticize the "working class" but this guy was the real thing. Perhaps we should have gone in there, torn up an office, knocked some heads...

We moved beyond the confessional phase and into something sloppier. He agreed to try things my way, to let the union pull him out of the fire. They'd done it for me. I trusted them.

I called our limo friend. He took us home for the cost of a tank of gas. Dropped off my co-worker first, in Inglewood, then took me south on the freeway to my house in Gardena. I was feeling that elated type of drunkenness, top of the world. I'd headed off a nasty situation and here I was, back seat of a big black Lincoln Continental, a labor leader. The airlines seemed intent on firing my co-worker.

Things went back and forth for a week or so. When the Airlines agreed to allow a grievance hearing I thought we had them on their knees. We still didn't have a contract, but management had agreed to negotiate and things seemed to be moving. Raises were coming soon, we were assured. The crew was happy—morale was high. I remember some great parties during that period.

We met with Ernie and the lawyer at a Marriott in Century City. Went over strategy—that the clocking in rule was a form of intimidation and that employees tried in good faith to show up on time. I was to argue the case but Ernie and the lawyer would be there to watch my back. Were they grooming me, or throwing me to the wolves? I'll never know.

The rules regarding the grievance process are pretty ambiguous, at least with regard to transportation workers. Common sense would call for an arbiter, or at least a referee. This was backroom stuff—a couple of union reps, management, the accused, maybe a witness. No rules of order—you scream it out. And management makes the final decision, or at least they did at that point since we had no contract. I blew up when Ernie sketched out the "rules" a few minutes before the meeting, but I calmed down. What could I do? The accused just shook his head, leaned over to me, said, "I'm getting out of this bloody fucking country."

That ride out from the terminal to the office in the blue and white tram then into a conference room that seemed too big for the occasion. We waited, then someone came in and said that the plans had been changed and that the meeting would be in Mr. Harlen's office. Down a hall and up one flight of stairs. Big window facing the Pacific. The beach, the ocean, big planes heading off toward Asia. Very nice. We waited awhile—such an obvious strategy but the obviousness makes it more effective. Something like, "this guy is fucking with me because he can." And the psych worked on me—I remember thinking, "we're dead." But Ernie chuckled and smiled that horizontal smile, said, "this is so fucking bush league."

Harlen came in looking like The President of the United States. I'd never seen an expensive suit close up but I knew he was wearing one. Tall, with graying temples. A Skycap had told me that he was once a ticket agent and that he'd worked his way up the ladder. I've learned since that they're the worst kind. Scab mentality. Think and grow rich, win friends and influence people. We all shook hands. I caught an eye roll from my defendant.

I mapped out my case and made my argument. Ernie backed me up but it seemed that his heart wasn't in it. Harlen didn't present any kind of argument. There was lots of sage-like nodding, ahems and uh-hums. At times he'd look out the window and nod, or follow the flight of a 747. I wanted to ask him what he was thinking but I didn't, I just kept talking.

First, I tried to show that a superhuman attempt was made to comply with the rules. I asked the accused a few questions, got the answers I expected, but there was no attempt to cross-examine, or whatever you'd call it in this situation. Then I questioned the rule itself. Harlen leaned forward, slowly, half-smiled, said, "but we make the rules, Mr. Hill." I got a blank look from Ernie. Instinctively I put a hand on my comrade's shoulder. I figured he'd blow soon. But he didn't. We'd been hung out to dry. I quickly reached that kind of anger where you feel steely and calm. This must be where people start shooting, I thought. Harlen straight at me, said, "Do you think I'm wrong, Mr. Hill?" and I felt, still feel, the ramifications. Morally wrong, destructive, evil, but correct in his statement.

They made the rules. But I looked back at him, said, "yes, you're wrong" and started a speech. Ernie cut me off with a look that could kill. Harlen said he'd "reach his decision" in a day or two.

The tram was usually a quiet place. I mean, it was noisy on the runway but people didn't talk much. They were on their way to or from work, that funny transitional time. Lean back, rest your head against the window and enjoy a few minutes of freedom. We probably made that tram pretty uncomfortable for the others—yelling at Ernie Mogg. A double tirade—me calling him a traitor and my friend bringing Kropotkin into the fight. Ernie waited it out, rope-a-doping us until we were out of insults. The word that seemed to wake him up was "scab." I don't remember who said it. He shook his head. No. He was big to begin with and he seemed to get bigger, and the lawyer, who had been playing the "I don't know these people" game, joined the fray. They'd both been through hell for the union, really, and they let us know it. Lost jobs and fistfights and jail time. The phrase I remember is "this is how we survive." They hated the game too but they knew how to play, and if we'd just shut up and listen…

A few days later Ernie called me at home. "Harlen's going to tell you that nobody will be fired over the rule, that he'd ease up on it. There will be a two week suspension without pay. When you talk to him, thank him." And he hung up. The call came and I did what I was told. My friend went back to England but his sister stayed on. She said she liked the States despite the sorry politics.

Contract negotiations dragged on for months but the intimidation eased off. Ernie would call occasionally and ask what I thought of this or that point. Mostly I agreed with him—happily surprised by some of the accommodations. They hadn't gotten around to flight benefits but the proposed raise was substantial, also more sick and vacation pay and a more structured grievance procedure. Finally I got the call that a contract could be signed. The union rented a large suite at the Marriott, really swank, and called staggered meetings so that the whole crew could show. I was given a sick day to stay all day. The contract was good, solid. It included back pay dating from the day we signed our cards. The flight discounts were small and hard to obtain. Still everybody, even the "scabs," voted yes. Money talks.

I was in the yard playing with the dog when the phone rang in the kitchen. I ran in to catch it—this was pre-answering machine. It was Ernie, sounding a little nervous. First the good news—the Op Manager had been fired. Then—and I'll never know how this was worked out—he said that my back pay would include severance pay, but that I really wasn't being fired, I could just call it a leave of absence and after a year or so I should call him and he'd fix me up with something. "Finish school, travel, have fun. Hell, you're barely twenty-one yet. Why work full time?" I decided in a second that I'd had it with the airlines. I must have been mad at Ernie but that's not what I remember most—I remember feeling relief, and a funny kind of pride. I'd been blacklisted. A real revolutionary!

I decided to drop out of school and travel until the money ran out. My last act as a lame duck was to call people and strongly suggest that my friend the Brit anarchist be elected the next steward. She was, and she raised hell, from what I heard.

The crew threw a nice goodbye party for me and I was presented with something that I kept for years—God, I wish I could find it now. Why didn't I frame it? Someone in middle management—I think I know who, but she never copped to it—had broken into the personnel files and found my application for employment. Scrawled across the front, in red letters: DO NOT REHIRE! UNION TROUBLEMAKER!

F. A. Nettelbeck

Hermosa was a surfer town, still is, but now the surfers work well-paying day jobs. They have to—property values shot through the roof in the '80s and they haven't come down much. In '76 I was sharing a house on Eighth Street—one of those cheap rent stories that old bohemians brag about. I was paying about a hundred a month for a nice room in a falling-apart beach house. Fireplace, enough of a yard for Emily, my lab mix, eight blocks from the beach and about three blocks from the bookstore.

I began my education in the Either/Or bookstore on Pier Avenue. I was attending classes at El Camino College and sneaking into others at Long Beach State (poets taught there), but I fed my head at Either/Or. Marx, Paul Goodman and I.F. Stone for my agitator side. McClure's *Meat Science* led me out of the mainstream—thank you, Michael. I'd come in from the bright LA light and hit the politics sections, check out the fiction section for Bukowski or Bowles, look at poetry—Wanda Coleman was a favorite then. But I gave these shorter shrift—I was headed back behind the register, to a dim lit (nice contrast to all that beachy sunshine) small press section. An alcove, really. Mimeo, local stuff, handmade limited editions. Issues of *Invisible City* edited by Paul Vangelisti and John McBride, a long poem, *The Burning of Los Angeles*, by Jack Hirschman, mimeo edition with illustrations. Bertrand Mathieu's translation of *Season In Hell*, intro by Anaïs Nin, illustrations by Jim Dine—I hear that translation in my head when I think of Rimbaud, "I sat beauty on my knee and I roughed her up..." SoCal poets some nearly forgotten—Locklin, Koertke,

Steve Richmond, Stephen Jama. But also some that went on to "bigger" publication—Amy Gerstler, Dennis Cooper, Tom Clark, Elaine Equi…

I don't remember the book, or the poem but at some point I stumbled onto F.A. Nettelbeck. Some permeation of *Bug Death*, in some mimeo, probably. I read it before I'd read Burroughs, possibly didn't know about cut-ups—I met Harold Norse a year or so later, I think. That's ok. I didn't need historical context to appreciate the poems. Either way they would have taken the top of my head off, as the poet said. His filtering process was scary perfect. The thing that most sours me on "experimental" poetry is that, with most, there are so many more misses that hits. Too much wasted time, too many wasted words. Too much ego—why did they leave that in? I think, as I try to read. Nettelbeck never wasted time. Staccato little lines, hard hitting, a film noir kind of feeling but not at all retro or clichéd: tribes rehearse the/ritual for the/videotaping/ (the raper.) forcing/pink legs apart after/this instinct settles/ slowly like mud into/a dried out skull. Leafing through his work now I'm amazed at its rigor. Rigorous isn't a word you'd usually associate with his "type" of poetry—the "road to excess" school. But, really, it takes a kind of stubbornness to stay on the road—it's a long way to the palace. The street signs fly by. Who can read them, let alone choose those that matter and set them down in discernable (sublime!) order? One hell of a job—a life's work.

Something like eighty percent of Americans see themselves as middle class, which is a lie of course, there's the oppressor class and then there's the rest. I think, among the "middle class," there's a sneaky realization of that lie, like an itch you can't scratch—or maybe a cancer. Some become more aware of the lie—and for some of us, at a certain age—late teens? Early twenties? There's this search for authenticity—often embarrassing—white boys trying to sing the blues. Most give it up—possibly not a bad thing—society needs ballast, and it's tough to keep up mortgage payments when traveling the road of excess. But I'm fascinated by those that stay true, or try. I've had long stretches on the road, but I've also stayed too long at the rest stops. Nettelbeck's work had that blues singer/jazz musician/pirate quality, fascinating yet embarrassing to the middle class. Should we leave it be and stay bland? Appreciate from a distance? Jump right in and risk a life on the outside? Authenticity is a tough nut.

warm alcohol glow known
as god we are almost
home they say repeat,
give me something
warm—your arms clinging

I was working at Logos Books and Records in Santa Cruz when *Americruiser* came out, early eighties. After work I'd go to the Teacup Bar, in an old Chinese restaurant on Pacific Avenue. The earthquake of '89 flattened the place. Nettelbeck drank there, but we didn't talk that much. We had a mutual friend, Bill Simmons, a visual artist and if Bill was there I'd join in on group discussions. Mostly, I think, Nettelbeck went there for quiet drinks—me too—so we sat at opposite ends of the bar. It's strange but kind of great to be immersed in the work of an artist, to see him or her in passing, watch from a distance. Possibly more to learn that way than from asking direct questions. He had a nice way with the bartenders—the Teacup hired young women, mostly of the punk persuasion. Those were Big Book years for me—athletic reading. Russian novels, Melville, lots of Gertrude Stein. And Joyce. A good way to go for a while, until it becomes like too much rich food. Nettelbeck seemed to chew that stuff up and spit it back out at you. Not that those others haven't stayed with me, and often nourished me—but, in a way, Nettelbeck has had a bigger effect. Or, more visceral at least—I saw what he was seeing. Living in Santa Cruz sans car meant taking Greyhound a lot, to San Francisco or Oakland to get a little taste of the urban. Nettelbeck sucked the poetry out of the greyhound rides, the stations, and all that "real" stuff. And, reading back the previous sentence I realize how clichéd it can seem—"the only ones for me are the mad ones." That searching for the real in the dark corners is, perhaps, an inauthentic practice for those who will probably return to the "middle class." And, yet, the alternative is to ignore what's going on—all that awful unruly stuff, all that depth. What's a middle class boy to do? I don't think Nettelbeck wrestled much with that one—he seems pretty aware that he's part of the oppressed class, probably never thought of himself as middle anything. At least, that's what his poetry says—more like, look at this sucker! Isn't that an interesting bug?

"I have talked to mentally crippled idiots, holding good jobs."

I imagine he never had a "good job." The road to excess probably doesn't allow for that. Another tough nut of an idea. Occurs to me that I'll probably never enter the palace of wisdom—I worry too much about my retirement.

I think beginning in the eighties his poetry just didn't get considered. I think people who did know about him saw him as a kind of Burroughs knock-off. I know they were pals, but I don't see too much overlap, stylistically. But, mostly, I don't think people of the eighties avant ilk read or thought about his work. I find this really fascinating—that he wasn't picked up by the avant or post-avant. There was a fork in the road, somewhere, and the cutting edge became less edgy, more refined maybe but the visceral was given a wide berth. There was a lower gross out factor. And the pros and cons of having a good job didn't get discussed. The cutting edge didn't threaten the man in the gray flannel suit. Real life issues were left out of focus—like trickle down or the foreign wars. Nettelbeck's poetry points to the elephant in the room. Hell, he scared me! To stretch the zoo animal metaphor, he was like those monkeys that throw their own shit at the patrons. Take that! The message being: I'm in a cage, fucker. Let me out! (or, Unscrew the doors themselves from their jambs!). This is dangerous stuff—enough to make most get off the road of excess at the next off-ramp. One good way to avoid the issue—marginalize the whole thing by declaring it out of fashion—or doing a Gertrude Stein—"that doesn't interest us."

Patti Smith

I could possibly get online and find the Rodney on the Roq show in, I think, summer of 1976 where Patti Smith says that she and Lenny are stranded in LA and need plane fare home and if Rodney could throw something together they would play, but mostly there would be poetry and that their fee would be one-way tickets home.

But this time I'll avoid the disappointment. I've listened to the Bob Marley late set at the Roxy, '75 and although it is excellent it doesn't, I guess obviously, cut as deep as it did, and I can't quite get the feeling of changing out of work clothes and waiting in line to get into the second show (no tickets, he wasn't such a big draw then) with a bunch of Jamaican guys from baggage service, LAX, and not caring that they were laughing at my attempt at dancing because I'm in total awe, wondering why that massive portrait of Haile Selassie anyway? You can't go back of course, but online info glut sometimes makes you think so before it lets you down.

We listened to two shows on KROQ every Sunday night, somebody called the Young Marquis followed I think by Rodney. My first exposure to Punk, earlier that year, probably singles from England and a few LA bands. A friend was going to shows but although I was interested it didn't yet fit my mid-seventies persona, long hair tied back and work boots, warehouse jobs, reading Marx and beat poetry, taking slow down drugs.

I was living in an apartment in Redondo Beach, '40s vintage, view of Fisherman's Wharf, a beautifully seedy waterfront back then, low rents and a five minute drive to Hermosa Beach, The Lighthouse, "LA's oldest jazz club and waterfront dive" or something like that (according to the radio ads). I was getting most of my music there, name a jazz musician (excepting maybe Miles) and I probably saw them, either barside or outside by the kitchen where you could listen for free with beach sounds in the background. I'd come home and my apartment mates would be listening to The Eagles or some such garbage but occasionally it would be Zevon, who for me was a kind of segue to appreciating Punk.

Sunday nights the stereo (the kind with fake wood and shit, speakers that took up the living room) belonged to my just-becoming-punk girlfriend, always ahead of the curve (with me trying to keep up). Rodney—Ramones, Sex Pistols, and LA bands (I loved The Weirdos right off. So funny and political). I guess the walls were thick, or the neighbors were deaf, or something. It just had to be loud enough to hurt. The drugs changed too. Some guy would come over, his opening line was always "the drugstore is open!" and then sleep became an avoidable annoyance. Our apartment mates either put up with us or went out, I don't remember.

Great to remember this now, without interference of the internet (but not going online is like not lighting up a cigarette when you really want one). Memories of lying on the floor Sunday nights, smell of the ocean and the traffic sounds drowned out by the music. Music like an anvil! Jesus died for somebody's sins…

It had to be summer because it was LA hot, even at the beach. The usual Sunday night music/drug cocktail. Rodney played something from, I remember distinctly, Radio Ethiopia, Ask the Angels (I had been playing Horses since it came out, and of course she was a poet, and the Mapplethorpe photo on the cover…) followed by a phone interview. Here in the realm of the beautifully vague I don't remember exact words, just the deep color of her phrasing New Jersey-cum-Rimbaud, that everything-I-say-is-poetry confidence, good God. How could any lover of language resist? I felt that total fandom feeling that too much sophistication tends to kill. Wallowed in it. Me and Lenny need plane fare home. Can you get us a gig? And by the end of the show they were booked, two blocks from my apartment, a bar called Sweetwater that featured mostly sensitive singer-songwriters and the occasional surf band. Down at the heels, fittingly.

Patti Smith in Redondo Beach. Did it happen? Patti, did you do this thing? And now I'm swimming in this kind of delicious thought that I'm making this up, but I don't think I am, but it could be the beginning of a story, just a fiction. Given time the things that didn't happen, or not, or that didn't get recorded, are the most satisfying, imagination being what it is, so full with deep embellishment.

And so I'm heading down to Sweetwater, white dress shirt and jeans because for some reason that was the uniform before the black torn clothes/buttons arrived. And the girlfriend had cut my hair and my face had that tight feeling that was brought on by certain drugs. Not walking, flying, but not floating either. Flying fast in a chosen direction. Speed of light.

Three poems into it the crowd is yelling for music but for me the words have done it, I'm never the same, God what a stupid thing to say but art lifts you up sure as a tornado and she was/ is a force of nature. I was never on the high road to "success" but until then had been confused by that, didn't know why. Three poems in I no longer cared.

Clifford Still

1.

I was between apartments and Simmons, a painter friend, knew another painter friend who had once dropped out of SFAI and had moved into a house in Santa Cruz, or actually out on the road to Felton. Simmons did what he jokingly called tchotchke art—gathering up trash and gluing it together. He'd gone to Davis and had lived in Humboldt—the kind of artist that drives a truck and listens to Merle Haggard.

The SFAI dropout was a different sort, I'd been told. He was following his wife to Japan, some sort of residency. Had dropped out of art school after a row with a painting teacher. This was years ago, when people were more apt to let big ideas interrupt careers. We could live cheaply, then, and MFAs didn't mean as much. He did big paintings that I probably wouldn't get. Or so my De Forest/Wiley trained friend said, with a smirk. I didn't take that well. I knew a little about art. I read High Performance, I went to openings, saw student films… Do you get them, Simmons?

I get them. I just don't like them. I'm not saying you're stupid—but he came up through minimalism and most of the canvases are like that, although now he's taken things in a different direction. More content. But probably just colors to you. Anyway they need a cat sitter and they're partial to poets. If you don't get the work just pretend it's the wallpaper—that's not much of a stretch.

I thought about arguing, but at that point I was playing Boswell to Simmons's Dr. Johnson. I let it go. He'd hooked me into a free place and all I had to do was feed a couple of cats. I was grateful.

The house was pretty ramshackle. Getting the toilet to flush was a real project, and the water was hot and then cold at minute intervals. The cats ran with raccoons and other small mammals—everybody used the cat door and shared the food bowl. The painter's wife did something with performance—pieces of costume were everywhere, things that were probably used as props, in that performance-artist/theater way. A kind of friendly squalor covered the floors and hid in the corners. But the walls!

You entered through a side door, the kitchen. No art there—then, around through the living area, the minimalist stuff. Gray-blue, big—the thing (I learned, looking for hours) about minimalist canvases is that they are always changing, not just with the light but with changes in mood, or whatever feeds perception. That speck becomes a bird, becomes a big idea, becomes...until there's this constant state of becoming, and then not, and back again. I'd play at naming the things that I "saw," as a writer that came naturally. And then, a state beyond naming. The paintings allowed me to go there—they had this openness.

There were a couple of bedrooms. No studio. I don't know where he painted.

The bedrooms had what I assumed was the newer stuff. He'd changed, completely. He was taking control. Through jagged lines and dramatic changes in color he pushed my brain where he wanted it to go. I never got to know him, have run into him a few times through the years. I didn't have the kind of information that might lead me to over psychologize, but I could see that he was coming to full power, flexing his muscles. The bedroom paintings possibly weren't as good, but I found, to my surprise at the time, that I was more drawn to them. Surprised, because at the time I thought of myself as leaning in some vaguely Zen direction—and here I was drawn to the more "western"—in that awful west coast pop usage of the word—type of art. Not so much balance—a knife fight! And I wanted to see more art like that, but even more dramatic—and the best of it. If you're going to free the doors from their jambs, I thought (had been reading Whitman), you have to push, pull, and kick...hard.

2.

The old SFMOMA on Van Ness was a strange-ass building for an art museum—galleries that looked like hallways, weird little side rooms, and that huge light filled center that was too big for just about everything. I loved it—so obviously inappropriate, but dramatic, and the shows were great. This particular visit we were going to look at the Manuel Neri that they had in the stairwell—no, really. It was just there on a landing, where nobody looked. A painted torso, pretty indicative of his work, which is to say, exquisite.

I told Simmons that I wanted to look at something big, dramatic and abstract.

Well you know the players. But the best stuff's in New York, except for the Stills.

They gave Still a room, off to the side, kind of on the way to the cafeteria. Bench in the middle, not too many paintings. And it was like a Sistine Chapel—that same catch in the breath and a dizziness. When I walk into places like that I'm grateful to be an atheist. Because, once free of theological baggage you clearly see the coupling of imagination and action that makes the work bigger than the one. From the artist, out…

3.

Frank O'Hara called him a force of nature. There's that ambivalence that comes out of the "artist as force of nature" idea. Oh, come off it…but then, how do you work big? You kind of have to think of yourself as big, too—involved in that struggle for immortality. Especially embarrassing, in these self-consciously unpretentious times.

I admit that I hate that the paintings aren't really titled. I'm a writer, I want a clue in words. I understand—the Grand

Canyon didn't name itself. But I'm bothered by it, and begin each looking "session" trying to name and describe before succumbing to awe.

I guess I'm in love with them ("I think I am in love with painting") and the struggle is part of that.

I look at those paintings and they beat me up—or I fight them, fight even appreciating them, fucking jags of color. There's a real abyss there, Grand Canyon sized drop—but also the possibility of flight. Reading interviews with Still—kind of opaque. Not much patience with other artists—their lack of integrity. But knew he was one of the great ones, so, here it is, take it or not. Makes me think that great art is always somewhere out beyond caring. The ocean does not mean to be listened to, as the poet said.

Difficult paintings, overwhelming, and cruel sometimes, but not stingy. Singular and great—is anybody doing that, now.

Frank Gehry Special

Via Nomentano is a nice hike from the historic center and has that urban neighborhood feeling that can allow tourists to think of themselves as travelers. I hadn't explored that area in previous trips. I once knew people near the Coliseum who would put me up for a couple of days then find me a room close by, so I mainly stayed there. Mostly when I'm there I am a tourist, wide-eyed, tripping over monuments, eating too much, acting as Fellini as is affordable.

This time we needed a little income. We had quit our jobs in LA to bum around and were doing ok before a couple of big blowouts in London and Amsterdam. In the days before we all carried our phones you would go to a post office to make a long-distance call. We snugged into a wood panel booth in Frieberg and I called Carla. She had some sort of translating job—she was always onto something—and the work needed "cleaning up." I have baby Italian and Nora spoke German, we'd be no help there, but don't worry, this was a rewrite job. Didn't you guys major in English?

Switching from German to Italian trains was stressful then, before the system became sleek. No seats so we sat on the floor or hung out in the snack bar but it doesn't matter how tired and cranky you are when you hit Rome you hit Rome and the rest of everything doesn't matter. Planet Rome. Fuck earth.

And so the set-up, talked fast while playing dodge-em with luggage carts and travelers in Stazione Termini then hailing a cab. Carla was having an affair (her word) with a brilliant architect whose wife was dying of a terrible disease, he was writing a book on California culture and needed "natives" to pepper the text with local color, a snap job and Rubino is really a delightful guy. There might also be some problems with transitions, punctuation, and that. Room and board, just past the Porta Pia, nice neighborhood.

I caught an eye roll from Nora. She only knew Carla very casually but sensed that we were entering the Carla zone and that drama would ensue. The tossed off detail about the dying wife did seem ominous but I wasn't going to worry about it. Worry seems inappropriate in Rome. It's a shut up and live kind of city. Just enjoy it. Even the goriest details seem superfluous there. Worrying would seem disrespectful to the culture. Drama is something to be discussed and enjoyed over the grappa.

The apartment was small but the room was ok. Carla's aunt Fani held the lease but a couple of other women either lived there or just hung out. The room was stripped down and a little cramped but that wasn't an issue. We said yes, settled in, went to check out the neighborhood.

Open market, pizza and gelato, espresso. Same old same old now in any city, not so then, and even now they do it better there. And, so, this works, let's stop for a Campari and watch the little cars go by, then take the bus into the center to see Carla, who has a room near the steps. We meet Rubino at dinner, pizza al funghi at a very crowded place, angling for tables the way the natives do, pushing and shoving. His English is slightly better than my Italian but it's noisy and we catch few words in the din. Carla tries to translate by shouting in my ear, then I play telephone and talk at Nora. I keep hearing the word post, as in (I learned later) postmodernism. Post this, post that. And something about Mussolini.

The pizza place was around the corner and in back of the Pantheon. We finished and walked through the square, Rubino post this and post that, pointing at buildings then asking us about California, but not understanding our answers. I tried answering in Italian, what a joke. We dropped him off somewhere, in a fog of mutual confusion, then headed back to Carla's place. That's a pretty great walk!

Carla tried to explain Rubino's book. It made no sense at all. It was the first time I'd heard of the heroes of Euro Pomo. Pick your favorite, he got quoted. I became aware that I was witnessing the dawn of something, but for the life of me I couldn't get interested. Soon the grappa came out and a painter friend came in, and the talk turned Roman—lovers, drama, the great paintings that he would paint. I felt closer to my element. Late, we left Carla with the painter, they apparently had something going, and took a late full bus back to Nomentano.

Next day, work. A place across the river from the Vatican. We were to meet them in front of Rubino's office. They were late, Carla's way. We went next door and loaded up with espresso. Carla found us. Rubino would be along soon, she had the keys to his office so we could get started.

The office was, I suppose, Post. The building itself was ancient by American (and especially Californian) standards and the furniture was a mix of modern and something that, at the time, I thought of as Disneyland. I surmised that Post meant mixing up stuff. Ok by me. Looking back, I suppose it was the beginning of what became the office-as-playground, that crap we have to endure now. Not quite a nursery school, but close.

Carla brought out copies of the manuscript, titled Frank O. Gehry, Special. Hard copy of course. A little early for personal computers, before the days of online editing. She left so that we could spend some time with the work. Since then I've picked up on some of this gibberish, even tried a reading group, but this was my first exposure. We traded off reading lines aloud and laughing. Figured it was just a bad translation. I thought about how to respond, about the politics of being with a new love and having to tell the old flame that the work was laughably bad. Now I've come to recognize that type of sentence, meandering and self-reflective in a way that could be playful but seldom is because humor isn't part of the game. There was a learning curve, I guess, but not much to be learned.

But we needed the room and board and we were ignorant of it all and so we decided to struggle with it. And we were in Rome. A few hours a day with rubber sentences was a small price to pay. He was placing the weight of theory on Gehry and his California, a carnival of dumbness. We peppered the text with California-isms, mostly ironically but who would know? Cowabunga!

And then we'd leave the office and it was like being let out of church. I don't remember the street but the river was right there casting dirty reflections and cooling things a little. You could see the layers of history, that thing about really old cities. Really grabs Americans—paved with rubble/ancient footprints are everywhere. And the residents get to play at not noticing, which also grabs Americans. A Roman friend, offering a tour, rolls her eyes and says "I suppose we should look at something old" and we follow Carla to the pizza place, pausing at the Pantheon. Then we're in an old building, not quite ancient, maybe 19th century, with "Eames" chairs and Buddy Holly covers playing. Ok the layers and I would appreciate that but thinking that Rubino got it, as a poet said, all New York complicated. Euro complicated. Am I a brute? Or a minimalist?

I've smoothed out some but I probably was or fancied myself like that and I miss that feeling now.

Rubino would arrive and we would talk at angles, not adept enough at each other's language. He had some beautiful misconceptions about SoCal and those ridiculous Gehry structures, filtered through French theory, with a little Euro arrogance thrown in. He would feast his eyes on Nora, a definite SoCal type, blonde and tanned, and she would blow him off in ways that were subtle and funny. Carla would get it, we'd laugh, and he'd puff up, and now I realize that we were also arrogant, the arrogance of youth.

I miss that too.

The walk after dinner was the best part. It's a good hike, from the Pantheon through the Villa Borghese (with a stop to take in the view of Del Popolo, the old churches and the ugly little cars) then out the other side of the park, past the Porta Pia and down Via Nomentano. Just Italy, just Europe. Streetcars and patina'd buildings in a line, smelly air. The layers are there but, after a while, not being aware of them heightens the appreciation. Without mediation of metaphor or symbol, as the poet said. Bumping the surface, and it isn't a mirror it's a wall but a nice old wall. Just appreciating it, the guy passing on the slow moving bus in a tight suit, the funny little cherubs flying off the sides of the buildings, the softness/grittiness of being alone together in a city that could swallow you up but who would mind? Grace to be born, state of grace.

The Caravaggio Trail

He called, come and see me. The hospital was only a few blocks from my place on Dwight Way. He wanted a Cap Grande. "They let you drink that much coffee?"

"They'll let me do anything I like." And I figured it was the end of the line.

There's an office building on Telegraph near Oregon St. and at the time it had an espresso cart in the lobby, there to pump up the attorneys and dentists before work and on break. I ordered one for me and one for him and walked another block and a half to the hospital. I had a cheap remaindered reprint of a Caravaggio in my bookbag, a Taschen reprint but not one of the gifty ones, a rough old hardback. I didn't understand why he might want that one. After years of obsession with the artist he had a pretty extensive library, but he was the ultimate obscurantist, there was possibly something setting this edition apart.

The drill wasn't new to me, the germ shedding washing entrance, the mask. The staff knew me and I assumed they were smiling behind their masks. Then into his room, a private room but I think they all must have been in this ward. There was a new nurse and he introduced me. Will was the type of person who got to know the workers, and it all seemed pretty natural, he'd stayed on his own job until the final months. Turns out the nurse was from West Africa, can't remember where exactly, but it touched off a friendly discussion of here vs there, of the differences in the languages even though we were all from English speaking places. The nurse was a poet, and I imagined Will digging that fact out of him because he was like that, always getting at your story. And so we were all poets, and bonded a little before the nurse left and Will said, as always, "take off the fucking mask."

The bed was littered with material for the Caravaggio book, bios and criticism and larger format, beautifully illustrated imported editions, and with notebooks of various sizes, the makings of Will's book. I never really saw it, except a couple of poems but it wasn't to be a book of poetry. Mostly we would talk about and around it, talk about which paintings he'd seen and what I'd seen. Once he mentioned, a little out of context, that all the old churches are dusky, the light is low, and when you turn on the little coin op lights the light shines on a painting not the cross, one of those things he would say when drifting, and the poetic drifting of the conversation would be infectious, the sort of thing that comes out of a certain level of inebriation, or late at night when your guard is down.

He wanted to see Boy Bitten by a Lizard and we leafed through the books. It's a tough one to find. There was an ok plate in an older, slightly beat-up Abrams edition. There's a version in London, we'd both seen that but the second, I think later version is in a private museum in Rome and only open to scholars. Will had made an appointment although he had no academic connections, had seen the painting which is a real nightmare, one of Carravagio's cartoons of fear, you see one of those things and your dreams change, are deeper and more disturbing. And he saw the painting and got on a train and spent one night in Florence, "unfriendly and shitty little town," and then trained down to Orvieto, his idea of paradise, and that night had wild boar for the first time. We riffed on wild boar, how it is milder than you'd expect, not so wild, but the taste has a subtle linger, like rabbit it tastes like almost nothing, then it tastes like—itself, nothing else. And from there, drifting, he was in Japan and somebody told him that the best sake had no taste or nose, like clear water, but if you drink sake you know that's what it is. Then back to Orvieto, appreciating in absence Boy Bitten by a Lizard, and this small epiphany he had about the painting and how it somehow zeroed in on a line by Martial, "Spare this lizard crawling after you treacherous boy/it wants to die between your fingers." And that he didn't know at the time that the painting was possibly inspired by the lines, and he had been reading Martial and the line came back to him as he was eating boar with red wine, outdoor restaurant overlooking a vineyard, "after dusk because they eat late." Then, "that lizard between your fingers. Scary as death, but warm at the underbelly, you love it until it kills you or you love it so you let it kill you, or maybe the bite is just a little bite and it gets you off."

Laughter sounds strange in a hospital, where the acoustics usually match the mood, thin sound bouncing off the walls and the machinery. People tend to lower their voices to a whisper, but we laughed ad alta voce and it felt good. He made a joke around "he who laughs last," good satisfying gallows humor, where the wave of humor subsides into darkness.

During earlier visits, in a different room, he was allowed to go outside to a terrace and take a smoke break but he was beyond that now. Didn't have that kind of mobility. He mimed a puff, missing it, his pleasures telescoping, focusing down to coffee, illustrations of his favorite paintings, conversation, writing. At least here he wasn't "hooked up" to all those machines, had some dignity, and probably because of this was in better spirits.

I looked, upside down at the scrawl in the notebooks and thought about my eye strain when it came time to transcribe the book. I was anxious to start but the rule was that I couldn't start until he finished, but did finish mean finished, that the project would be, or that he would be, and then I felt guilty for wanting to get started on it, not knowing the definitions of finishing and starting.

"And not to sink into metaphor"—he distrusted yet loved metaphor in poetry, this was an old note for us to touch on, and a look could convey my response. We shared the expected smile and he went on, about the light at dusk in Orvieto, and that sent me off on my own, another locale, another dusk, but also somewhere in that part of the world. And, from him, "ok what is it" and "it" was a lunch in Compenero or Compeneno, the memory isn't specific until I zero in on the lunch itself, ok don't think Proust, I only know about Proust from talking to Will. We were lost on a bus outside of Rome, got off at the wrong stop, wrong town. The usual, pasta with oil, strong meat dish, dark red wine, unselfconsciously rustic, impossible to do in the Bay Area where we know too much (even remembering it presumes too much), and lunch went on so long that dusk came on before coffee. His eyebrows still raised. "Compenero, or was it Compeneno," and he got it from that.

"But back to Caravaggio." He worked with his pillows a little and pulled another book closer. The Fortune Teller, not one of my favorites. The pose had a Dutch Master quality, too precious. We hadn't talked about that one. Had he been writing about it?

"I don't know who is the greater sorcerer/the woman you paint/or you who paint her. Who's the poet? A contemporary, or close. Can't remember. Damn morphine. But you can see it here (pointing to the page), the rest of the poem is almost a kill the messenger. The artist in cahoots with the grifter, and so makes the grift more dangerous. Romanticising the sorcerer."

Discussion of The Grift was another touchstone, "never give a sucker an even break, never smarten up the fall guy," the idea of "putting one over," the idea that that was the essence of art, except when it wasn't and when it wasn't, "like in Carravagio's best," it becomes, as Brecht said (sometimes blurted out together), "when I say what must be said everyone's heart will be torn to shreds," and then laughing at the utter pretentiousness of our talking like that, and the delight in that, as a way of sneaking up on, or crawling up to, the facade of art then the lack of a facade, if it could ever lack a facade.

He wanted another coffee. It was a short walk down to the office building and I needed some air, but could he handle more caffeine? He caught my worried look and waved his hand. I knew what he needed, I mean the kind of drug he needed. We liked and hated the same drugs, had been "speed freaks" together, maybe thirty years ago. I knew, from my own health problems that pain drugs were the worst, that there was this need to break through, feel some energy. And so I went out for the caffeine, the way I might have once gone out for some other drug, waiting on a bench overlooking the ocean in Santa Cruz, up by the Dream Inn. At least this was easier than that. It was a nice day for a walk and the cafe was open. Double Cap for him, decaf for me. I'm careful about everything now.

He had a poem he wanted to show me, about the Seven Works of Mercy. I wondered if we'd get to it. He hadn't really shown me anything, we just talked, looked at paintings, read background material. No complaints. His work, his game, his deathbed. He took a good sized gulp of coffee, shuddered. Did it make him cold? I reached over and pulled the blanket up for him, not the sort of thing I'd usually do, although we always, going way back, hugged warmly when meeting, but that wasn't the true source of our tenderness, it came with the lowering of our voices, mostly.

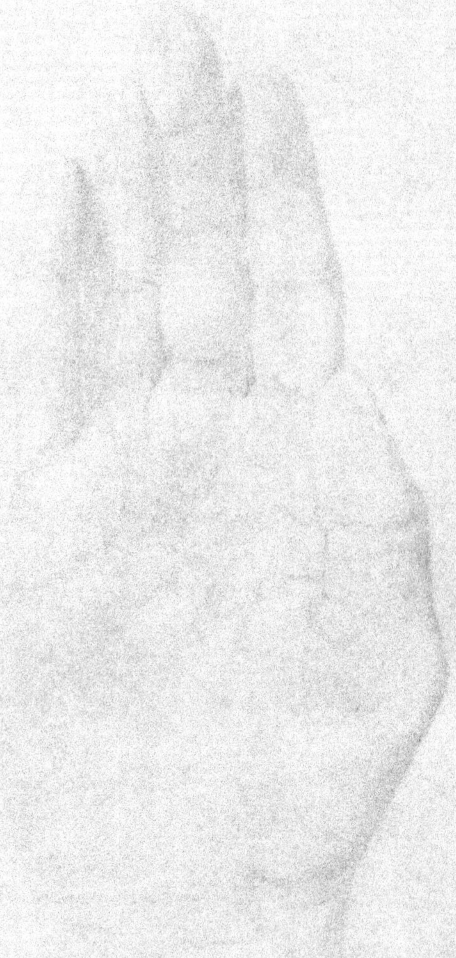

CPSIA information can be obtained
at www.ICGtesting.com
Printed in the USA
LVHW032153200322
713942LV00003B/77

9 781946 741097